Jet Pilot

By Geoffrey T. Williams
Illustrated by Nixon Galloway

PRICE STERN SLOAN
Los Angeles

The author wishes to thank the following people who helped to make this book possible: from the United States Navy, Captain Mike Ranftle, Commander (retired), Squadron #VFC13, Miramar Naval Air Station, who spent many hours with me making sure the cockpit language and fighter sequences were as authentic as possible; Captain Mike Rishel, who helped get it all off the ground; from USAir, Flight 236, Captain Steve Salmonsen and First Officer D.K. (Don) Buffington, Jr.; Flight 215, Captain L. Patrick Kewley and First Officer Jerry Leugers; Operations, Pat Flynn and Phillip Freedman; for the flight announcement, flight attendant Terri Skill; and I especially wish to thank Ms. Agnes Huff, Vice President, USAir Corporate Communications, Western Region—the jumpseat flight she arranged was a special highlight.

Copyright © 1992 by Geoffrey T. Williams
Illustrations copyright © 1992 by Price Stern Sloan, Inc.
Published by Price Stern Sloan, Inc.
11150 Olympic Boulevard, Suite 650, Los Angeles, California 90064

ISBN: 0-8431-2928-X (book and cassette)
ISBN: 0-8431-3365-1 (book only)

10 9 8 7 6 5 4 3 2 1

"Flight recorder?"
"Set."
"Cabin pressure?"
"Set."
The pilot and copilot were flipping switches and checking instruments, getting the Boeing 737-300 ready for takeoff. The engines were whining, the radio was crackling, the whole plane was humming like it couldn't wait to get off the ground. I knew just how it felt.

I've wanted to fly airplanes ever since I can remember. I've read about planes, built models of planes and dreamed about planes. But that's all I ever did until Dad came home from his business trip.

"Chris, I talked with the pilot of the plane I was on, and I told him how much you want to fly. Know what he said?"

"What?"

"He wanted to know if you'd like to fly with him."

My mouth dropped open. "What did you tell him?"

Dad grinned. "What do you think I told him?"

So here I was, sitting in the jumpseat behind the pilot and copilot in the cockpit of a Boeing 737-300 about to take off. I fastened my seat belt. In the passenger cabin behind me, the flight attendants were welcoming people on board. On the cockpit radio I heard air-traffic controllers in the control tower giving landing and takeoff instructions to other planes. A few minutes later it was our turn.

"Flight 236, you are cleared to taxi runway two-seven."

First Officer Carrera, the copilot, answered, "Roger, tower. Two thirty-six taxiing runway two-seven."

The pilot, Captain McDunn, nudged the throttles forward. The engines whined louder as we rolled toward the runway.

"Good morning, ladies and gentlemen. Welcome aboard Flight 236, with service to San Francisco." A flight

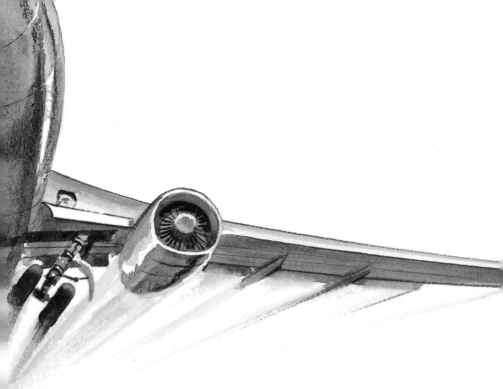

attendant was giving passengers instructions about emergencies and safety regulations. Through the windshield I saw a jumbo jet taking off in front of us. We were next.

"Flight 236, you are cleared for takeoff, runway two-seven."

Captain McDunn gave the engines more throttle. They revved louder and faster. So did my heart. "Roger, tower. Two thirty-six taking off runway two-seven." Then he gave it full throttle. The engines thundered. The plane shuddered. As the brakes were released, it leaped forward. I was pushed back against my seat. What power! Buildings and trees flashed past.

First Officer Carrera called out our speed, "60...80...110...130...rotate."

The cabin tilted sharply as Captain McDunn pulled back on the wheel. The runway fell away beneath us. We were flying!

"Landing gear up."

"Roger."

"Flaps up."

We climbed into the bright sky. The hands of the altimeter whirled around, showing how high we were flying—12,000 . . . 15,000 . . . 18,000 feet.

"Climb checklist complete," Captain McDunn said.

Carrera flipped some switches and set some dials on a wide panel in front. "Engaging autopilot." Now the computer was flying the plane.

Captain McDunn turned on his microphone to talk to the passengers. "This is
your captain speaking. Welcome aboard
Flight 236 to San Francisco. We'll be cruising
at an altitude of 35,000 feet at about 500 miles
an hour. Flight time will be just over an hour. Flight attendants will be serving beverages and snacks in just a few
minutes...."

"How can something as big as this airliner fly?"

"The way any airplane flies, Chris. With lift and thrust. Lift helps the plane overcome gravity, the force that holds things to the ground. And thrust helps the plane overcome drag. Drag is air resistance. When you stick your hand out the window of a moving car, the wind pushes against it the same way it pushes or drags on an airplane."

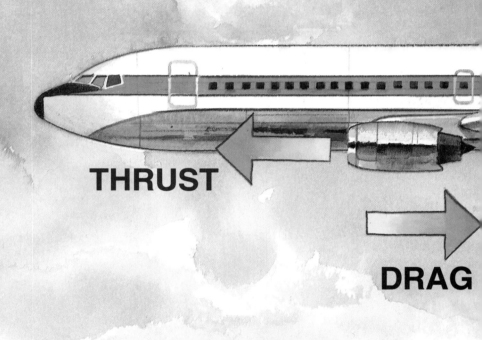

THRUST

DRAG

"How does the plane get lift and thrust?"

He pointed outside the window. "Thrust comes from those big jet engines pushing us."

"And propellors pull the plane, right?"

"Right. Now, lift's a little tougher to explain, but basically it comes from the special shape of an airplane's wing...curved on top and straight on the bottom."

"What does that do?"

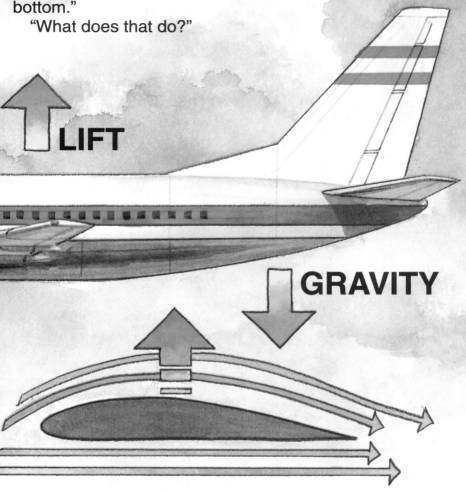

"That causes air moving across the top of the wing to go faster than air moving across the bottom. The people who design airplanes know that fast-moving air has low pressure and slow-moving air has high pressure, and that high-pressure air flows into lower pressure air. Since the high-pressure air is underneath the wing, it pushes the wing up."

"Once you're up, how do you steer?"

"By using the plane's control surfaces: the ailerons, rudder and elevator. The ailerons and rudder turn the plane. Ailerons are on the back edge of the wing near the tip. They move up and down with this control wheel." He tapped the wheel in front of him. "The rudder is on the vertical tail. It moves back and forth when I push these two foot pedals." They were where a brake pedal on a car would be. "Turning the wheel to the left moves the left aileron up and the right one down, and pushing the left foot pedal moves the rudder to the left. That's how you make a left turn in the sky."

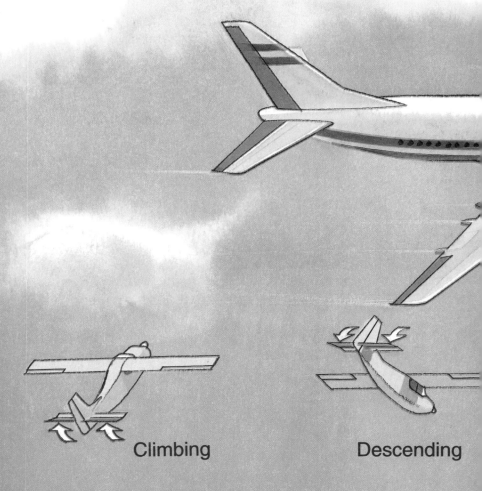

Climbing   Descending

"What about the elevator? What does it do?"

"It's the small horizontal wing-shaped part of the tail section, below the rudder. It moves with the control wheel too. Pulling back raises it, causing the plane to climb. Pushing on the wheel lowers the elevator, causing the plane to descend. Or, as pilots sometimes say, 'When you pull back, the trees get smaller. When you push forward, the houses get bigger.'"

I laughed. He made it sound simple, but I knew better.

Turning right   Turning left

"Cabin pressure."

"Set."

"Flaps five degrees."

"Selected."

"Flight 236, you are cleared for landing. Runway two-eight left."

"Roger. Two thirty-six cleared for landing, runway two-eight left."

"Landing gear?"

"Three down and locked."

Just as we were getting ready to land, the collision-avoidance alarm went off and I nearly jumped out of my skin!

"Traffic! Traffic!" a computer voice warned. It automatically goes off if there's another plane close by. The Captain and First Officer immediately searched the sky.

"Traffic! Traffic!"

This could be serious. Then Carrera spotted it. "Helicopter."

I saw it, too. A mile or so to the left and above us. Probably from one of the radio or TV stations. No problem. I breathed a sigh of relief.

Below us, buildings and parked planes lined the field. Cars looked like tiny models. Skyscrapers towered in the distance. The hills were green and beautiful. I could see it all. Bridges and boats and islands and ocean. I had the best seat in the plane.

Then we were busy landing. The runway rose to meet us. The wings dipped and tilted slightly as Captain McDunn made tiny movements of the wheel to keep us level. There was the slightest bump as we touched down. The engines roared as the Captain put them into reverse thrust. The giant plane began to slow.

A few minutes later we taxied to a stop outside the terminal and the passengers began getting off. It was a routine flight. Nothing out of the ordinary. But that's the way a good pilot and crew make it feel.

"We've got some time before we refuel and get ready for the return flight. How would you like to try my chair on for size?" Captain McDunn asked me.

I couldn't believe my ears! "Sure!"

I climbed into the seat. "Put this on." He handed me his headset with the earphones and microphone he used to communicate with the control tower. Then he handed me his captain's hat. I put it on. It was too big but I didn't care! I put my hands on either side of the control wheel. It felt warm. And it was pulsing like a giant, living creature. I was feeling its heartbeat. I closed my eyes. So this is what it really feels like, I thought. This is wild. "How can I get to be a pilot?"

"A lot of pilots get their training in the military. I'm a reserve jet pilot at Miramar Naval Air Station—" He stopped and looked at me. "Say, how would you like to see some fighter jets?"

What do you think I told him?

"This is where the Navy trains its Top Gun pilots," Captain McDunn shouted over the roar of jet engines.

"Are they the best pilots in the Navy?"

He grinned. "We like to think they're the best in the world, Chris."

"What kind of jets are those?" Three planes with long, thin needle-noses and twin tails were getting ready to take off a few hundred feet away.

"F-18 *Hornets*. The Navy's newest fighters."

The lead pilot opened the throttle and let the brakes off. Waves of thunder rolled across the field as the jet started down the runway. The ground shook. The sound beat against my body.

Wow! I thought. Nothing can get any louder than this! Then the pilot turned on his after-burners. Flames shot out the exhaust with an explosion of noise, and the *Hornet* screamed down the runway! The pilot pulled back on the stick and climbed so steeply it looked like he was riding a ball of fire. The other two streaked into the sky right after him. Then they disappeared into the clouds.

"Wow! How fast can they go?"

"Almost Mach 2—twice the speed of sound. Close to 1,200 miles an hour."

"1,200 miles an hour!" What would it be like flying something that fast?

TOP GUN
FIGHTERTOWN, U.S.A.

"This is Shooter. Request clearance to Air Combat Training Area."

"Roger, Shooter. You are cleared to Air Combat Training Area. Climb and maintain 25,000 feet."

The Miramar control tower looked out over the whole airfield. Down at the end of the runway I saw two F-14s ready to take off.

"This is Lightning. Ready for takeoff with two Tomcats."

"Wind 250 degrees at 5 knots. You're cleared for takeoff runway two-four right."

"*Roger. Cleared to go. Rolling two* Tomcats." The windows of the tower shook as the two-man fighters blasted off.

"Where are they going?"

"Out over the desert for air combat training."

"You mean a dogfight?"

"Want to watch?"

"You bet!"

The room was dark except for the big, bright computer screen—like a giant video game. On it I could see six planes: the two F-14s and four smaller jets.

"There are two A-4s and two F-5s playing the part of the enemy fighters," Captain McDunn said. "Computers on the ground and on the planes are sending back information so the instructor here can see how they're flying."

"Is this a real fight?"

"No. None of the planes have real missiles or ammunition. But the computer lets us see what would happen if they did."

The instructor was wearing a headset and talking into a microphone. "This is Midnight. I've got four bogeys at twenty-two miles. Closure 1,200."

"What's that mean?"

"He just told the F-14s that there are four enemy planes twenty-two miles away. Closure is how fast they're flying toward each other—1,200 miles per hour. At that speed they'll be on top of each other in about a minute."

"This is Shooter. I got a good lock on the leader."

"That's the RIO—the Radar Intercept Officer—the second man in the F-14. Lock means radar has sighted the enemy plane, and they're ready to fire a missile."

"This is Lightning. We've got three contacts—two different locks."

"And there's a guy behind them," Midnight said. "I show four, repeat, four bogeys."

I heard a beep of sound.

"Fox 1 from Shooter."

"Shooter just pretended to fire a Sparrow air-to-air missile," Captain McDunn said. On the screen the computer drew a box around one of the A-4s.

"One down, Shooter."

"*Fox 1 from Lightning.*"

There was a beep.

"That's one for you, Lightning."

"*Fox 2 F-5.*"

"Shooter just pretended to fire a Sidewinder missile at one of the F-5s."

"*Let's go, Supersonic!*" Shooter's after-burners screamed as his *Tomcat* turned and roared away at more than 1,000 miles an hour. *"Did we get 'em all, Midnight?"*

"You got one F-5 left. He's angels 10 at 8 miles."

"Angels 10 means 10,000 feet altitude," said Captain McDunn.

"*Okay. Lightning, let's go back and get this guy.*"

"Fox 2 from Lightning."

"That's a miss, Lightning. A miss."

There was a high, warbling tone, and then Shooter's voice. *"He's got a lock! Bogey's got a lock on me! Help me out, Lightning!"*

"Where is he?"

"I can't see him!"

Suddenly I felt as nervous as Shooter sounded!

"Midnight, you got him?"

"Ten o'clock high!"

"Tallyho!"

"Get this guy, Lightning!"

"Fox 2!"

On the computer screen, the Sidewinder streaked toward the enemy plane at more than 2,000 miles an hour. A second later a little box appeared around the F-5. And that was it. It was over in less than two minutes.

"Good one. You got 'em all. Let's knock it off," Midnight radioed.

"What's your call sign going to be?" Captain McDunn asked me.

"I'll have to think about that one."

"Well, while you're thinking, try this on for size." The flight helmet was too big. But so what? This was the real thing. An F-18 *Hornet.* And I was sitting in the pilot's seat! I could smell hot jet exhaust and hear the roar of other fighter planes close by. I was excited. And nervous. And sweaty. I felt wild! And then I knew—when I really got my wings—I knew what my call sign would be.

"Tower, this is Wildcat requesting takeoff."

"*Roger, Wildcat. You're cleared for takeoff, runway two-four right. Wind 205 at 10 knots. Climb and maintain 40,000 feet.*"

"Roger, tower. Rolling one *Hornet*." And the engines thundered as I roared into the sky.

Explore the farthest reaches of our world and beyond with book and audiocassette packages from Geoffrey T. Williams and Price Stern Sloan!

Loaded with facts and fun, each book is full of realistic color illustrations. Action-packed audiocassettes tell the story word for word, and sensational music and explosive sound effects recorded in three-dimensional sound put you right in the middle of the action!

Adventures in the Solar System

Dinosaur World

Explorers in Dinosaur World

Hello, Mars!

I'm a Jet Pilot

The Last Frontier: Antarctica

Lost in Dinosaur World

These books, and many others, may be bought wherever books are sold, or may be ordered directly from the publisher. For further information call 1-800-421-0892.

Price Stern Sloan, Inc.
11150 Olympic Boulevard, Suite 650
Los Angeles, California 90064